Twins

Janet Olearski

About this Book

For the Student

Listen to the story and do some activities on your Audio CD

End of the listening excerpt

Talk about the story

beat• When you see the blue dot you can check the word in the glossary

K Prepare for Cambridge English: Key (KET) for Schools

For the Teacher

HELBLING e-ZONE THE EDUCATIONAL PLATFORM A state-of-the-art interactive learning environment with 1000s of free online self-correcting activities for your chosen readers.

Go to our Readers Resource site for information on using readers and downloadable Resource Sheets, photocopiable Worksheets and Answer Keys. Plus free sample tracks from the story.

www.helblingreaders.com

For lots of great ideas on using Graded Readers consult Reading Matters, the Teacher's Guide to using Helbling Readers.

Level 3 Structures

Present continuous for future	Cardinal / ordinal numbers
Present perfect	*One / ones*
Present perfect versus past simple	Reflexive pronouns
Should / shouldn't (advice and obligation)	Indefinite pronouns
Must / should	
Need to / have to	*Too* plus adjective
Will	*Not* plus adjective plus *enough*
	Relative pronouns *who, which* and *that*
Ever / never	Prepositions of time, place and movement
Would like	
So do I / neither do I	
Question tags	

Structures from lower levels are also included

Contents

Meet the Author

Hello, Janet, can you tell us something about yourself?
Yes, I'm originally from London. I grew up and went to school there. My mum was English and my dad was Polish, which is why I have a foreign-sounding surname. I've lived in several different countries and now my home is in Abu Dhabi, which is in the United Arab Emirates.

What are your hobbies?
My favourite hobbies are reading and horse riding. I like animals. I have a cat whose name is Bandit, a parrot who is called QuackQuack – Quackie for short – and five tortoises, who are called... 'tortoises'. Let me know if you can think of names for them.

Your story is called *Twins*. Do you have a twin brother or sister?
No, I don't have any brothers or sisters, but I've always wondered what it would be like to have a brother or a sister who looked like me. In fact lots of brothers and sisters don't look like each other at all.

What gave you the idea for this story?
My favourite uncle was called Uncle Frank. He worked in the movies• as an actor and a stunt• man. He was an amazing character and he always had a good story to tell me. I based *Twins* on one of those stories and I made my dear old Uncle Frank a character in the book.

Why did you write this story?
I wanted to show that honesty is the best policy•. Telling lies can make your life very complicated.

Glossary

- **movies:** films
- **policy:** (here) thing to do
- **stunt:** acrobatic tricks or actions

Before Reading

1 **Look at the pictures of these identical twins. Are they really identical? Can you spot five differences between them? Tell a friend. Use the words below to talk about the pictures.**

a) 

b) 

hair eyes face nose eyebrows ears mouth
round small large straight curved wide
brown blue freckles dark light

2 **Choose six chapter titles from the Contents list on page 5. Work with a partner or in a small group. Make up a short story based on your six chapter titles. Tell your story to another group.**

3 **Look at the pictures below. Describe what you see.**

4 **Which is the best place to go on holiday, and why? Discuss with your partner.**

Before Reading

1 Match the words with the pictures.

a) marker pen
b) tortoise
c) arch
d) fountain
e) trunk
f) bench
g) handbag
h) poster

1 

2 

3 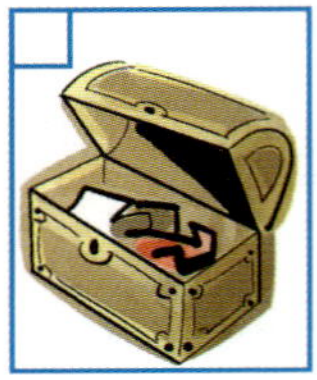

4 

5 

6 

7 

8 

2 Now use these words to complete the sentences below.

a) The gardener went to sit on a .... and ate his sandwiches in a shaded corner of the park.

b) Claire's lunchbox was dripping wet after the boy threw it into the ....

c) Tim put up .... all around the school.

d) Someone drew over the school posters with a yellow ....

e) Mrs Green had all her money in the .... that the man stole from her.

f) A .... is a reptile-like creature with a hard shell.

g) William was swinging like a monkey from a wooden .... at the entrance to the rose garden.

h) Uncle Frank found his photographs inside an old ....

3 **Look at the pictures. Imagine what the characters are like. Compare with a partner.**

Tim's mum

Mrs Barrow

Tim

William

4 **The central character in *Twins* is a boy called Tim. You can see him in the picture above. What do you think he is like? Write down four questions to ask him. Ask your partner to answer the questions.**

a) ....

b) ....

c) ....

d) ....

Before Reading

1 Look through the pictures in the book. What do you think *Twins* will be about? Tick (✔) the boxes below.

a) ☐ A horror story about good and bad.
b) ☐ A story about a woman who is going to have twins.
c) ☐ A story about twin brothers.
d) ☐ A story about twin sisters.
e) ☐ A story about two young people who meet and fall in love.
f) ☐ A crime story.
g) ☐ Something else. Tell the class.

2 Here are some people from the story. What do they do in the book? Decide in pairs.

a) ☐ 

b) ☐ 

c) ☐ 

d) ☐ 

1 She pretends she is Tim's mother.
2 He likes telling exciting stories.
3 He thinks that Tim is a hooligan.
4 She decorates Arkwright with lots of art.

3 Read these sentences. Do you agree with them? Circle a number.

1 = I don't agree at all.
5 = I totally agree.

a) Mothers always know when their children are hiding secrets.

1 2 3 4 5

b) Young people can learn a lot from old people.

1 2 3 4 5

c) People only obey the law because they are afraid of getting into trouble.

1 2 3 4 5

d) You need a lot of good luck to pass exams or win awards.

1 2 3 4 5

e) If children behave badly, it is the fault of their parents.

1 2 3 4 5

f) If your friend is in trouble, it's fine to tell lies to help him/her.

1 2 3 4 5

g) Boys shouldn't cry.

1 2 3 4 5

h) You need a good memory if you tell lies.

1 2 3 4 5

4 On page 6, in Meet the Author, Janet says:

"honesty is the best policy."

In groups think of examples to show that this is true.

MILK

MUM IN A HURRY

2

'Got to rush. Will you be OK?'

As usual Tim's mum was in a hurry. She had so much to do and so little time. She gathered up• her car keys, her house keys, her phone, her bag, her books.

'Mum, slow down,' said Tim.

'See you at 4pm,' said Mum. 'I'll meet you at the fitness centre•. Don't forget. We're going over to see Auntie Ruby and Uncle Frank at the new house.'

'Mum, you need a holiday.'

'Yes, I do, darling,' said Mum, 'but not today. Remember to switch off• the lights and lock the door. Love you. Bye.'

And she was gone. She was like a whirlwind•.

Tim finished his bowl of cornflakes and thought how his mum was really the best Mum in the world. She worked so hard. She took care of him, she had a job, she was studying for a degree, and she looked after Uncle Frank. She should actually get an award•: the Best Mum of the Year Award. Yes, she should get an award, a cheque for a large amount of money, and a wonderful holiday. A holiday where?

Busy People

Who is the busiest person in your family? Describe what they do on a typical day.

Glossary

- **award:** prize
- **fitness centre:** gym; sports hall
- **gathered (up):** picked (up); took
- **switch off:** turn off
- **whirlwind:** fast, powerful wind

THE AWARD

'Disneyland Paris? You're not serious!' said Tim.

'Yes, I am,' said Jenny. 'Someone has donated• money to the school for a Student of the Year Award.'

Tim, Jenny and William were waiting for morning assembly• to start. Everyone around them was talking about the Student of the Year Award.

'I don't believe it,' said Tim. 'Who's going to give us a heap• of money just to go on holiday and have fun?'

'It's an incentive•,' said William.

'What do you mean?' said Tim.

'Well, we have to think of a good idea to help the school,' said William. 'If it's a really great idea, then we could win the Student of the Year Award and then we win a trip to Disneyland Paris.'

'How many people can go?'

'I don't know,' said William, shrugging• his shoulders. 'Two maybe. Don't worry, Tim. If you win, it's OK for you to take me.'

'Not likely•,' said Tim.

'That's enough talking,' said Mrs Barrow. Arkwright School's new Head Teacher was standing on the stage• in front of them. 'Can I have your attention, please?' she said. She was a small plump• woman with a very powerful voice. When she spoke, the children fell silent.

'I'm sure you have all heard about the new Arkwright School Student of the Year Award. Basically, we want you to think of an original activity that will benefit• the school and the local

Glossary

- **a heap:** a lot
- **assembly:** meeting
- **benefit:** be useful to
- **donated:** given; made a gift
- **incentive:** motivation; reward that encourages you to do something
- **not likely:** definitely not
- **plump:** a little fat
- **shrugging:** moving up and down
- **stage:** raised area for actors, singers, etc.

community,' said Mrs Barrow. 'Once you think of an idea you have to write a proposal• – your teacher will help you – and submit• it to our Student of the Year Committee. Whoever thinks of the best idea for a project will get our Student of the Year trophy• and a family ticket for four people to Disneyland Paris.'

'That's it,' said Tim. 'I'm going to be Student of the Year.'

'Yes, you and two hundred others,' said William.

The children were all talking now and it was very noisy.

'And, I haven't finished talking yet, thank you,' said Mrs Barrow. There were a few shrieks• of laughter and then the children were silent again.

'In addition to writing the proposal, you actually have to do the project. We want to see results, not just ideas. You must show us how your project benefits the school or the community, or both.'

One or two children started to talk again. Mrs Barrow raised her hand.

'Some announcements,' she said. 'Number one. Don't throw litter• around the school and especially not in your classrooms. Some of the teachers are complaining•.'

'All of the teachers are complaining,' whispered William.

'Sssh,' said Jenny.

'Number two. Please pay at the office if you are going ice skating on Saturday.'

'Brrr. Too cold,' said William.

'William. Shut up!•' said Tim.

'And, number three, one important thing from the police.

- **complaining:** saying that they don't like it
- **litter:** rubbish
- **proposal:** plan
- **shrieks:** shouts; screams
- **shut up!:** be quiet!
- **submit:** give
- **trophy:** award

There have been reports of thefts• and muggings• in the Wrightham area, and one of our students has lost his phone. Possibly someone stole it. So, please be vigilant•. Report• any suspicious• behaviour to your class teacher, to me, or to the police, and please don't try to catch the thief yourself.'

'You behave very suspiciously, Tim,' said William. 'I think I'll report you.'

'Thanks, William,' said Tim. 'I'm glad I've got a friend I can depend on!'

Crime

Have you ever seen someone commit a crime? What happened?
Imagine you see a mugging. What do you do?

Glossary

- **muggings:** attacking someone to steal from them
- **report:** (here) say
- **suspicious:** when you feel someone is doing something bad
- **thefts:** when things are taken/stolen
- **vigilant:** observant; wide awake

INCIDENT AT THE GYM

As Tim stood with his bicycle outside the Parkside Fitness Centre, his head was full of plans for his holiday in Paris. Now he had to think of a project to win the award.

His mum came to the fitness centre to use the Parkside gym two or three times a week. The rest of the time she was at her job teaching at the local college or studying for her Master's degree• at the university. She was on her own•. Tim's mum and dad separated and divorced when he was five. Tim's dad was in New York now. He was married again and he had a second family. Tim thought about that for a minute. It was so weird• to think that maybe he had a step brother• who looked like him. Or maybe his step brother didn't look like him at all. It was just something he fantasized about•.

Brothers and sisters

Do you have any brothers or sisters?
Do they look like you?

Sometimes Tim felt sorry that his dad wasn't around•, but most of the time he didn't think about his dad at all. He had Mum, he had Auntie Ruby, he had Uncle Frank, he had lots of other relatives and he had his friends. And Mum looked after everyone. That's why a holiday in Paris was just what she needed.

- **around:** (here) close; in the area
- **fantasized about:** imagined
- **Master's degree:** university qualification
- **on her own:** alone
- **step brother:** a half brother (he has the same father as Tim but a different mother)
- **weird:** strange

Fitness
Centre

Lost in his thoughts, he didn't notice the tall thin dark-haired man who came rushing out of the gym. Tim heard the gym door open, he turned to see if it was Mum and collided head on• with the running man. Everything crashed to the ground: Tim's bike, his schoolbag, the man's sports bag.

Schoolbags

You probably have lots of different things in your schoolbag.

Work in groups of three.
Try to guess five things that each person has in their schoolbag.

'Sorry, mate•,' said the man. The two of them were on the ground picking up all the books and objects that had fallen onto the pavement. 'Didn't see you,' said the man. 'I was in a bit of a hurry.'

'No problem,' said Tim, but then he noticed the scratches• on the paintwork of his bike. He looked up to say something, but the man was gone. He looked down the street and saw the man disappearing into the distance.

'Hey, what happened to you?' said Mum. Tim was still down on the pavement trying to reorganise the contents of his bag.

'You look like you just got hit by a tornado•.'

'How did you know that?' said Tim.

'Mums know everything,' said Mum.

Glossary

- **collided head on:** crashed directly into (someone or something)
- **mate**: (slang) friend
- **scratches:** marks
- **tornado:** strong wind

BOXES

Uncle Frank's new house was very close to the fitness centre. His old house was in the middle of the country and Mum and her cousin Ruby convinced him to move into the town.

Uncle Frank hated the idea because he was very independent. But it was much easier for Mum to keep an eye• on him here in the town. Auntie Ruby, his daughter, lived in Scotland and she couldn't visit very often. There was a good doctor a few streets away and the shops were close by. There was even a social club for seniors• if he wanted some company.

Seniors

Which services are the most important for an old person to have close to their home? Choose three of the following and compare your choices with your partner's choices.

- [ ] A fitness centre
- [ ] A social club
- [ ] A restaurant
- [ ] A doctor's surgery
- [ ] A supermarket
- [ ] A hairdresser

'Thank goodness you're here,' said Auntie Ruby when they arrived. Tim looked around: there were boxes everywhere. The new house was in chaos•, and Auntie Ruby was in a state of panic. Outside there was a large van and men were carrying more boxes from the van into the house.

Glossary

- **chaos:** confusion
- **keep an eye (on):** watch
- **seniors:** old people

'It's a disaster,' said Ruby. 'I don't know where anything goes and I have to climb over the boxes to get into the rooms.'

'Where's Uncle Frank?' said Mum.

'I don't know,' said Ruby. 'I've lost him.'

'I'm over here,' shouted Uncle Frank. 'I'm behind these boxes in the living room.'

'Tim, do me a favour,' said Mum. 'Go and find your uncle Frank and see if he needs anything.'

'Yes,' shouted Uncle Frank. 'I need a cup of tea.'

Tim found Uncle Frank behind a wall of boxes, sitting on a large brown trunk•. In front of him was a stack• of old books.

'There you are, Uncle Frank,' said Tim. 'A nice cup of tea, just the way you like it.'

'Good boy!' said Uncle Frank. 'I knew I could rely on you. Come and look at these.'

- **stack:** pile; with one on top of the other
- **trunk:** suitcase like a large box

Tim sat down on one of the boxes and looked closer. The books were photo albums.

'I found them in the trunk,' said Uncle Frank. 'I forgot they were there.'

He turned the pages and pointed to a set of faded• yellow photographs. 'Look,' he said. 'That's me when I was your age.'

In the photos Tim saw a tall thin boy in a checked jacket and shorts. In one photo the boy was holding a rabbit. In another he had his arm around another boy's shoulders and was he smiling widely at the camera.

'That's awesome•!' said Tim. 'But you look a bit cheeky• to me. Look at the way you're smiling in this photo.'

'You're quite right,' said Uncle Frank. 'I was very naughty•. I was a terrible troublemaker• but when I got caught I just blamed everything on my identical twin brother.'

'I didn't know you had an identical twin,' said Tim.

'Ah! That's the point. I didn't,' said Uncle Frank. 'You see, a twin brother is very useful, even if he doesn't exist. If you do something wrong, you can always say it was your identical twin brother.'

Glossary

- **awesome:** amazing; wonderful
- **cheeky:** not well behaved
- **faded:** not clear
- **naughty:** bad
- **troublemaker:** person who does bad things

'I never thought of that,' said Tim.

'Well, think about it,' said Uncle Frank.

'Don't go giving him silly• ideas, Uncle Frank.' Mum was looking down at them from the top of the boxes. 'Here,' she said, handing• Tim some biscuits. 'I've brought you some supplies. That's enough chatter• for today. Uncle Frank, you and Auntie Ruby are staying with us until the house is ready.'

'Anything you say, boss,' said Uncle Frank.

'You know,' said Uncle Frank when Mum had gone, 'I hope you appreciate• your mother. She's a great person. Make sure you do everything you can to look after her. You're the man in the family after all.'

'I'm planning something very special for her, Uncle Frank. I'm going to take her to Disneyland in Paris.'

'My goodness! How are you going to do that?'

'Very simple, Uncle Frank. I'm going to be the Arkwright School Student of the Year and that's the prize: a trip to Disneyland.'

Uncle Frank punched• Tim on the arm. 'Good work, my man,' he said. 'I like your spirit!' Then he paused and gazed• for a moment into the distance. 'You know,' he said, 'I'd like to be Student of the Year myself, but I'm far too old for that now.'

- **appreciate:** understand how good someone is
- **chatter**: talking
- **gazed:** looked for a long time
- **handing:** giving
- **punched:** hit (someone) with your hand
- **silly:** stupid

Tim wobbled• and slipped• on the cold ice of the skating rink.

'I don't think ice skating is your thing•, is it?' said Jenny.

'It's good to try something new,' said Tim, 'but I think I prefer running. I'm good at that. Skating seems a little dangerous to me. Lots of people are falling over.'

Something new

Tim is not afraid to try something new.
Can you think of something new that you want to try?

'Come with me,' said Jenny, and she guided Tim along the ice. 'Let's talk about the award,' she said. 'Have you thought of anything?'

'Yes, I have,' said Tim. 'I want to start a KAT project.'

'I thought you preferred dogs,' said Jenny.

'K – A – T, not C – A – T, Jenny. KAT stands for• Keep Arkwright Tidy. I'm going to clean up the school. What do you think about that?'

'Wow! I'm impressed,' said Jenny.

'With me?' said William. He skated up beside them.

'I'm impressed with Tim's project,' said Jenny. 'I don't think mine is as good as that.'

'Probably not,' said William.

'Well, thanks for the encouragement•, William,' said Jenny.

Glossary

- **encouragement:** when you give someone hope
- **I don't think ice skating is your thing:** you're not very good at ice skating
- **slipped:** fell
- **stands for:** represents; means
- **wobbled:** moved unsteadily as though he was going to fall

NOT JUST A PENCIL CASE

5 'Tim, what are you doing?' said Jenny. 'You're not listening to me.'

Tim was busy looking in his schoolbag.

'Sorry, Jenny. I lost my pencil case,' said Tim. 'It's not just the pencil case, my money was in there and my favourite pen.'

Lost things

Have you ever lost anything that was important or special to you?
What did you lose?
Can you describe it?

'Did you leave your bag lying around anywhere? Maybe somebody stole your pencil case,' said Jenny. 'Don't worry, our good friend William will pay for our snacks today. Won't you, William?'

William grunted•. 'Oh, all right,' he said.

'And now,' said Jenny, 'This is my plan. I want to set up a club called Arkwright Art and I want to decorate the school walls with students' paintings and drawings and photographs, too.'

'And sculpture and pottery•,' said Tim. 'I can give you some of my pots.'

'Bad idea,' said William. 'People will call it AAA – Awful Arkwright Art.'

- **grunted:** made a sound that showed he was not happy
- **pottery:** ceramics like vases and plates, etc.

Behind them two girls burst out• laughing.

'It's OK,' said William. 'It's only Claire and Lynn.'

'We're leaving now because we have work to do on our project,' said Claire.

'We feel a bit sorry for you,' said Lynn, 'because your ideas are so pathetic•.'

'What are you going to do?' asked Tim.

'We can't tell you,' said Claire. 'It's a secret. You might steal our idea because it's so good.'

Jenny, Tim and William watched in silence as Claire and Lynn left the cafeteria whispering to each other and giggling•.

'What are you going to do, William?' said Tim, changing the subject.

'CiA,' said William.

'I don't like the sound of that,' said Jenny.

'Citizens' Aid,' said William. 'I'm going to do good deeds•. You know, help old people to cross the road and do their shopping. Things like that.'

'In that case we need to warn• people,' said Tim. 'I'm not sure that William is the right person for that job.'

'Very funny,' said William. 'I don't care if I don't win. I don't need to go to Disneyland to have fun. I can have lots of fun here at home. Think about it. Aren't there lots of things you would like to do, but don't do because you might get into trouble?'

'You mean like walking on the grass when it says "Don't walk on the grass"?' said Tim.

'Or ringing doorbells and then running away?' said Jenny.

'You are both so boring,' said William. 'Where is your imagination?'

Glossary

- **burst out:** (here) suddenly started
- **deeds:** things you do
- **giggling:** laughing in a childish way
- **pathetic:** useless; silly
- **warn:** tell people about something dangerous

THE SHOPPING TROLLEY

'Big shopping today, Tim,' said Mum. 'We're cooking for four – you, me, Uncle Frank and Auntie Ruby.' Tim and Mum were on their way to the supermarket.

'And Jenny and William,' said Tim. 'They're coming to work on our projects and we're short of• biscuits and cakes.'

'I'll buy you some nice healthy fruit then,' said Mum.

Tim frowned•.

Outside the supermarket Mrs Green's dog Bluebell was tied up and waiting for her owner. Jenny was kneeling beside her.

'Good dog,' said Jenny waving a half-eaten doughnut at her.

'Hello Tim. Hello, Mrs Norris,' said Jenny. 'I'm bonding• with Bluebell.'

'Grrr,' said Bluebell.

'There's a mugger about,' said Jenny, 'and it's important to keep Bluebell safe.'

'Let's hope that the mugger will be safe from Bluebell,' said Mum as she went into the shop.'

- **bonding:** trying to make a close relationship with someone
- **frowned:** made an expression to show he is unhappy
- **we're short of:** we don't have much/ many of

Jenny waited until Mum was out of earshot•.

'Have you seen William?' she whispered•. 'You won't believe it. He's started working on his project. Come and have a look. He's inside the supermarket.'

Jenny and Tim went through the automatic doors and down the aisles•, through the fruit and vegetable section and then to the tinned foods.

'There!' she said and she pointed.

'What?' said Tim. He couldn't see anything strange.

Old Mrs Green was looking at the shelves with great care and attention. She lifted down a tin, examined it and put it back it on the shelf. Then she took another tin, read the label and returned it to the shelf, too.

'Good afternoon, Mrs Green,' said Jenny. 'I was just wondering•. Do you need any help?'

'Hello, dear. No, I'm fine. It's just so difficult to decide what to buy these days. There's so much choice.'

'Do you need anyone to push your trolley•?'

'That's very kind of you, my dear, but this lovely boy has offered to help. Now where is he? William! William!' she called.

Just then a trolley came round the corner. It was moving very slowly.

'Is that trolley too heavy for you, William?' said Jenny.

'Surely not,' said Mrs Green. 'Come along, William, I haven't finished my shopping yet.'

William had a look of despair• on his face.

Glossary

- **aisles:** corridors
- **despair:** without hope
- **out of earshot:** far away (where he or she cannot hear)
- **trolley:** cart for food in a supermarket
- **whispered:** said in a low voice
- **wondering:** asking myself

HOME
TINNED FOOD
SALE
PEAS
BAKED BEANS
FISH

'Look at me,' shouted William. 'I bet you can't do this.'

William was swinging• like a monkey from a wooden arch at the entrance to the rose garden.

William

Work with a partner and make some notes about William. What do you know about him?
What three adjectives do you think describe him well?
Give reasons for your choice.

'Get down, William,' said Tim. 'The gardener will see you.'

'Come on, Tim. Don't be scared•,' shouted William.

'I'm not scared. It just looks...'

Glossary

- **scared:** afraid
- **swinging:** moving like a monkey while hanging

Before Tim could finish speaking, there was a loud creaking• sound. The wood started to bend. Then, the arch broke completely and William was on the ground with the wood lying in fragments• all around him.

'It just looks... a bit dangerous,' said Tim.

'Ouch!' said William.

'William, you've broken it! You've broken the arch. You're going to be in really big trouble.'

'Don't worry,' said William. 'It's not a big deal•. These things happen all the time. Now it's your turn, Tim. I dare• you. What are you going to do?'

'Nothing,' said Tim.

'Come on, Tim. You never do anything. You're just too scared. You've got to do something.'

- **big deal:** serious problem
- **creaking:** sharp sound (when wood is about to break)
- **dare:** challenge; ask someone to do something bold or that takes courage
- **fragments:** small pieces

Mr Thomas the gardener was busy planting flowers. He stepped back to admire his work. The park's lawn• looked fresh and green. He switched on the sprinklers• and watched the water rise into the air and spray• the grass. He picked up the sign that said, 'Don't walk on the grass!' and he put it by the path so that everyone could see it. Then, he picked up the brown paper bag with his sandwiches and he went to sit on a bench in a shaded• corner of the park.

He was just halfway through his first sandwich when he saw a boy standing on the edge of the lawn. The boy was probably about thirteen or fourteen years old. He was wearing jeans and a T-shirt. The boy looked first to the left and then to the right,

Glossary

- **lawn:** area of grass
- **shaded:** not in the sun
- **spray:** cover with drops of water
- **sprinklers:** machines for watering grass and plants

and then he stepped right onto the grass. Mr Thomas stood up. His bag of sandwiches fell to the ground.

'Hey, you,' he shouted. 'Get off my grass.'

The boy ran. He ran right across the wet grass. Mr Thomas ran after him waving• his arms in the air.

'Get off the grass this minute,' he shouted. But then his feet slipped and he fell down on the wet lawn. And the boy ran away.

Mr Thomas struggled to his feet. He was covered in mud. He looked at the ground and all he could see were the huge prints• and skid marks• left by his rubber boots.

'I'll get you!' shouted Mr Thomas. 'I know which school you go to. I'll come and find you!'

- **prints:** marks left by shoes or feet
- **skid marks:** marks on the ground when someone or something falls
- **waving:** moving (through the air)

GOOD WORK

7 'Stop worrying,' said William. 'He'll never report• you in a million years.'

William and Tim were going into morning assembly along with all the other students. Tim looked around him for signs of trouble•, but everything seemed normal. Mrs Barrow began with the Student of the Year projects.

'There are a lot of excellent projects,' she said. 'I'll mention• just a few of them today.' She paused for a moment. 'Claire and Lynn, can you please stand up?'

Claire stood up and smiled at the students around her. Lynn stood up, but turned red and stared at the floor.

Body language

Lynn turns red because she is embarrassed.
Think about what people do when they are:

- ☐ bored
- ☐ confused
- ☐ telling a lie
- ☐ feeling guilty

'Claire and Lynn have started a Reading for Kids project. Good work, Claire and Lynn. Jenny, can you stand up, please?' Jenny stood up. 'Now, all those pictures and items of artwork• on display around the school are part of Jenny's Arkwright Art project. Well done, Jenny!'

Glossary

- **artwork:** pieces of art
- **mention:** say
- **report:** complain about; tell some about
- **trouble:** problems

'William,' said Mrs Barrow. 'Where are you, William?'

William opened his eyes and stood up.

'William is helping old people in the community through his Citizens' Aid project. A truly excellent idea. I wish everyone would care for others the way William does.'

'Tim Norris,' said Mrs Barrow. Her voice was serious. Her expression was serious. 'Will you please come to the stage?' Tim's heart pounded•. He looked at William but William looked away. Tim stood up and walked to the front of the school hall. The other children stared at him as he climbed the steps of the stage and walked to where Mrs Barrow was standing.

Tim looked down at his trainers. They had mud and grass on them. He wanted to hide his feet.

'I want everyone here to take note of what Tim has done,' said Mrs Barrow. 'In just a very short space• of time, he has cleaned up the whole school as part of his KAT project. Now every class has a KAT person and the school is litter-free. Thank you, Tim.'

All the students and staff clapped• their hands. Tim gave a huge sigh of relief•.

- **clapped:** hit their hands together to thank
- **pounded:** beat like a drum
- **relief:** happy because a difficult moment passes
- **space:** (here) period

TERRY
THE TORTOISE

Mr Graham was late for class that morning. By the time he arrived, the children were laughing and talking at the top of their voices. Mr Graham looked pale and upset. The students fell silent immediately. They knew something was wrong.

'Tim,' said Mr Graham, 'could you please go to Mrs Barrow's office. Go right now,' he said.

'Yes, this is the boy,' said Mr Thomas. He was sitting in Mrs Barrow's office. He glared across the room at Tim. 'He's the one who trampled my flowers and who broke the arch in the rose garden.'

'No, it's not true,' said Tim.

'Are you quite sure, Mr Thomas?' said Mrs Barrow. 'Tim is one of Arkwright's very best students. Perhaps you are confusing him with someone else.'

'It's definitely him,' said Mr Thomas. 'In my opinion he's just a hooligan with no respect at all for public property.'

'Tim, is this true?' said Mrs Barrow. 'I really will not tolerate misbehaviour, and particularly from someone who wants to be our Student of the Year. What have you got to say for yourself?'

'It wasn't me, Mrs Barrow,' said Tim. 'Really it wasn't.'

'And, if it wasn't you, who was it?' said Mrs Barrow.

'It was... It was...'

'Yes?' said Mrs Barrow.

'It was... my brother,' said Tim.

'Your brother?'

'My twin brother,' said Tim.

Mrs Barrow and Mr Thomas stared at Tim open-mouthed.

Glossary

- **at the tops of their voices:** very loudly
- **glared:** looked angrily
- **hooligan:** a person who destroys things for fun
- **misbehaviour:** bad behaviour
- **pale:** white
- **tolerate:** accept; allow to happen
- **trampled:** crushed; stood on and destroyed

A TORTOISE CALLED TERRY

8 Mrs Barrow looked at Tim with suspicion. 'You've got a brother? I didn't know that.'

'Yes, Mrs Barrow.'

'What's your brother's name?'

'It's... It's...'

'Yes?' said Mrs Barrow. On the wall behind her was a child's drawing of a green reptile-like creature• with four legs. Underneath the drawing were the words, 'Terry the tortoise'.

'His name's Terry, Mrs Barrow.'

'I see,' said Mrs Barrow. 'And which school does Terry go to?'

'He goes to Crossbridge School, Mrs Barrow.'

'Let's phone them,' said Mr Thomas. 'What's their number?'

'One thing at a time, Mr Thomas,' said Mrs Barrow. She turned to look at Tim. 'Why doesn't Terry come to school with you, Tim?' said Mrs Barrow.

'Because,' said Tim, 'he doesn't live with us, Mrs Barrow. I live with our mum and he lives with our dad.'

'Oh!' said Mrs Barrow and Mr Thomas at the same time.

There was a moment of silence. Mr Thomas exchanged glances• with Mrs Barrow.

Tim's twin

What does Mrs Barrow find out about Tim's brother? Write three sentences about him.

Glossary

- **creature:** animal or reptile
- **exchanged glances:** looked at each other

'Tim,' said Mrs Barrow, 'can you please wait outside. I need to talk to Mr Thomas.'

It was a disaster. Tim felt that this must be the worst day of his life. He was in an impossible situation and he didn't know how to get out of• it. Now he had a brother, and his brother had a family and a life of his own. And he went to Crossbridge School, and in his spare• time he did bad things. And his brother's name was Terry. Terry the tortoise. The door of Mrs Barrow's office opened and Mr Thomas came out. He looked at Tim and shook his head then he walked away down the corridor.

'Tim, you can come in now,' said Mrs Barrow. 'I need to talk to you about this situation with your brother,' said Mrs Barrow.

'I'd rather not discuss it, Mrs Barrow,' said Tim and he bowed• his head. 'It makes me feel very unhappy,' he said.

Mrs Barrow's cheeks turned pink. 'I understand how you feel, Tim,' she said, 'but I need to meet your twin brother and talk to him.'

Tim did his best to look sad.

'I think I need to talk to your mother,' said Mrs Barrow. 'Can you please ask her to come and see me? Will you do that, please, Tim?'

'Yes, Mrs Barrow,' said Tim and he stared at the floor.

'Now, don't be upset, Tim. Would you like me to write her a note?'

'No,' said Tim, 'I'll tell her myself.'

'Very good,' said Mrs Barrow. 'Any day this week after 2pm will be fine.'

- **bowed:** bent his head down
- **get out of:** solve (a problem)
- **spare:** free

POOR TIM

It was the lunch break and the boys were playing football. Tim stood watching them with his hands in his pockets.

'Tim, is it true?' said Jenny. 'I can't believe you didn't tell us.'

'What?' said Tim.

'About your twin brother.'

'What?' said Tim.

'Don't keep saying "What?"' said Jenny. 'We're your best friends and you didn't tell us that you had a brother.'

'Who told you?' said Tim.

'Claire heard Mrs Barrow talking to Mr Graham. Everybody knows about it. Except me. I was the last person to find out and I'm your friend.'

William was standing by her side studying his nails.

'William, say something!' said Jenny.

William kicked at the ground with his trainers. Jenny turned round and faced him. 'William, did you know about Tim's twin?' she said. 'Did you know about this – what's his name? – Terry?'

'Well,' said William.

'Did you?' said Jenny.

'Yes, I did,' said William, 'but Tim wanted to keep it quiet•. Terry is not a nice person, you see.'

'How do you know that?' said Jenny. 'Have you met him?'

'I'm guessing,' said William.

'So why didn't either of you tell *me*?' said Jenny.

Getting annoyed

Why is Jenny annoyed with Tim and William?
Is she exaggerating?
Imagine you are Jenny.
How do you react?
Was there ever a time when you got angry or annoyed with one of your friends?
What happened?

'I was too ashamed•,' said Tim.

'He was embarrassed,' said William.

'That's right,' said Tim. 'You have no idea what it's like to have a black sheep• in the family.'

Behind them they heard voices.

Glossary

- **ashamed:** embarrassed
- **black sheep:** person in a family who behaves very badly
- **Tim wanted to keep it quiet:** Tim didn't want to tel anyone about it

'Auntie Ruby,' said Tim, 'I need your help. I have a problem.' Auntie Ruby looked up from her newspaper.

'Do you remember how Uncle Frank pretended to have a twin brother?' said Tim.

'Yes,' said Auntie Ruby.

A plan

What is Tim going to ask Auntie Ruby?
How do you think she will react?
Discuss with a partner.

The following afternoon, Auntie Ruby and Tim drove to Tim's school.

'I think this is a terrible idea,' said Auntie Ruby. 'I really don't want to do it.'

'You can wear Mum's hat,' said Tim. 'I brought it with me.'

'I don't want to wear your mum's hat,' said Auntie Ruby. 'This is not a wedding• I'm going to.'

Auntie Ruby had parked her car outside Arkwright School, but now she refused to get out.

'Please,' said Tim. 'Please, Auntie Ruby.'

'You should just tell the truth, Tim. Just tell them you ran across the grass. What's the problem? I don't understand.'

'But they think I broke the arch and I didn't.'

'Then tell them you didn't,' said Auntie Ruby.

'But now they think my twin brother did it.'

'That's your fault, Tim. Tell them you made a mistake and told a lie.'

'Mum will kill me if she finds out,' said Tim.

'Your mum will kill me if she finds out,' said Auntie Ruby.

Tim was in a state of despair•. 'Mum is looking after Uncle Frank,' he said, 'but you won't look after me. It's not fair.'

Auntie Ruby sighed. 'Oh, all right,' she said. 'Let's do it and get it over with•.'

What do you think?

What is Auntie Ruby going to do?
Do you think she is doing the correct thing?

Glossary

- **get it over with:** finish it
- **state of despair:** very worried
- **this is not a wedding:** female guests usually wear special hats for events like weddings

DIFFICULT QUESTIONS

10 'Mrs Norris?'

'Er, yes, that's me,' said Auntie Ruby as though she wasn't quite sure.

'You're Tim's mother,' said Mrs Barrow.

'Yes, I'm Tim's mother,' said Auntie Ruby.

'Yes, she's my mum,' said Tim.

'Thank you, Tim,' she said. 'Can you wait outside while I talk to your mother?'

'It's OK. I'll just sit here,' said Tim, taking a seat in one of Mrs Barrow's comfortable armchairs. He folded his arms and smiled.

'I'd prefer to speak to your mother in private,' said Mrs Barrow.

Tim gave Auntie Ruby a warning look.

'Oh, it's fine with me if Tim stays,' said Auntie Ruby. 'I don't have a problem with that.'

'Very well,' said Mrs Barrow. 'Now, there seems to be a problem with Tim's brother. He has misbehaved and even damaged some property.'

'Oh dear, oh dear, that's very bad,' said Auntie Ruby. 'I'll talk to him and erm...'

'Pay for the damage,' said Tim.

'Will I? Oh yes, I'll pay for the damage,' said Auntie Ruby. 'I'll make sure it doesn't happen again. Is it a lot of money?'

'To be honest, Mrs Norris,' said Mrs Barrow. 'I was not aware that Tim had a brother. I understand that he goes to Crossbridge School.'

'Oh, does he?' said Auntie Ruby. Tim glared• at Auntie Ruby. 'I mean, yes, he does,' said Auntie Ruby. 'That's right.'

Glossary

- **glared:** looked in an angry way

'Can you tell me why Terry doesn't come to Arkwright?' asked Mrs Barrow.

'Who?' said Auntie Ruby.

'Terry... your other son. Tim's twin brother.'

'Oh yes, Terry,' said Auntie Ruby, suddenly remembering her other son. 'Well, it's like this, Mrs Barrow,' said Auntie Ruby. 'I am divorced. And Tim lives with me, but Tom lives with his father.'

'Tom? Don't you mean Terry?'

'Yes. Terry. That's right. My son, Terry... who is the brother of Tim. Of course.'

Mrs Barrow looked concerned•. 'Would you like a glass of water, Mrs Norris?' she said.

Tim could see that the meeting was not going well. Mrs Barrow continued to ask Auntie Ruby questions. Tim watched the faces of both women. It was a bit like being at a tennis match. He noticed that Auntie Ruby was growing very red in the face. When Mrs Barrow turned her back, Auntie Ruby looked at Tim and mouthed• messages at him, messages like, 'Help me!' and 'Let's go now!' But then Mrs Barrow turned around and fired• another question at her.

'One thing really puzzles• me,' said Mrs Barrow. 'I don't understand why Tim and Terry always wear the same clothes. They both have the same yellow T-shirts, for example, and the same blue trainers.'

'My brother is very poor,' said Tim.

'Poor?' said Mrs Barrow.

'Yes,' said Tim. 'My dad lost his job so...'

'That's right,' said Auntie Ruby. 'His father doesn't have a job.'

Glossary

- **concerned:** worried
- **fired:** (here) asked
- **mouthed:** moved her lips to form words without making sound
- **puzzles:** confuses; is a mystery

'So they haven't got any money?' said Mrs Barrow.

'That's right,' said Auntie Ruby. 'I try to help Tom.'

'Terry,' said Mrs Barrow.

'I try to help Terry,' said Auntie Ruby.

'Mum buys two of everything,' said Tim.

'I buy two of everything,' said Ruby. 'One shirt for Tim. One shirt for Terry.'

'One pair of trainers for me and one pair of trainers for Terry,' added Tim. 'When she buys jeans for me, she buys jeans for him. I've got a pair of green socks and he's got a pair of green socks. I've got a yellow T-shirt and he's got the same yellow T-shirt. I've got a brown jumper and he's got...'

'I think Mrs Barrow has understood, Tim,' said Auntie Ruby.

Mrs Barrow sat down at her desk. She took a deep breath, put on her glasses and looked at a piece of paper in front of her. Then she took off her glasses and looked up. Her eyes were red and watery•.

'That's very sad,' she said. 'Very sad indeed.
Leave it with me,' she said. 'I'll explain the situation to Mr Thomas.'

Mistakes

Can you find three mistakes that Auntie Ruby makes in the meeting with Mrs Barrow?

• **watery:** with water in them (because she is sad)

Auntie Ruby winked• at Tim. Tim smiled back and looked out of Mrs Barrow's window. On the playing field his classmates were running about and having fun. Soon the story of his troublesome• twin would be behind him.

'Poor Terry,' said Mrs Barrow. 'From time to time we have cases like this of disruptive• students. I usually try to talk to both parents to find out the problem. I think I need to talk to Terry and Tim's father.'

Tim swung• round and looked at Mrs Barrow in horror.

Glossary

- **disruptive:** who cause trouble
- **swung:** turned quickly
- **troublesome:** difficult; who causes problems
- **winked:** made a sign with her eye, signalled

'My dad?'

'His father?' said Auntie Ruby.

'Your husband. Your ex-husband,' said Mrs Barrow.

'He's not here,' said Tim.

'No, that's right,' said Auntie Ruby. 'He's not here.'

'Where is he?' said Mrs Barrow.

'He's travelling,' said Tim.

'Travelling?' said Mrs Barrow.

'He's a travel writer,' said Auntie Ruby.

'He's an airline pilot,' said Tim.

Mrs Barrow looked confused.

'He's an airline pilot who writes about travelling,' said Auntie Ruby.

'He writes travel books? But you said he didn't have a job,' said Mrs Barrow.

Tim looked at Auntie Ruby with panic in his eyes.

'That's right,' said Auntie Ruby slowly. 'He was an airline pilot, but he lost his job and so...'

'Yes?' said Mrs Barrow.

'And so he can't write any travel books right now because...'

'He isn't visiting any interesting places,' said Tim.

'So he's got nothing to write about,' said Auntie Ruby.

'Right,' said Tim.

Mrs Barrow leaned forward in her chair. 'But you said he's travelling,' she said.

'Yes,' said Ruby, and she paused. Mrs Barrow and Tim waited. 'He's travelling to a job interview,' said Auntie Ruby.

'In New York,' said Tim.

'Ah!' said Mrs Barrow.

'Look at all this litter outside the school.'
'I think it was Terry.'

'Yes, it was definitely Terry.'

'Hey! Someone took my calculator.'
'It must have been Terry.'

'Has anyone seen my football scarf?'
'It was Terry. He took it. I saw him.'

'I can't find my mobile.'
'I bet• it was Terry.'

The accusations against Terry upset Tim. After all, he thought, Terry was his only brother, his twin. Terry was his closest and dearest• relative.

Blame

What things is Terry blamed for?
Has anyone blamed you for doing something that you didn't do?
What happened?
What did you say?

Glossary

- **bet:** (here) am sure
- **dearest:** most loved

Police are looking for a man in connection with a series of muggings and robberies in the Wrightham Park area. If you know this man or have information about his whereabouts, please contact the Wrightham Police.

The children were looking at the poster on the wall outside Wrightham Library.

'Your brother is causing a lot of trouble, Tim,' said William.

'Terry's really famous now,' said Lynn. 'He's quite muscular, isn't he? I suppose he works out,' she said.

'Not like you, Tim,' said Claire. 'You're skinny.'

'It's a very bad picture,' said Jenny. 'You can't see him.'

'I think he looks interesting,' said Lynn. Then she, Claire and William ran off.

'He doesn't look like you at all,' said Jenny and she turned to look at Tim. 'Do you have any photos of you and Terry together when you were babies?' she said.

'I don't know,' said Tim. 'I'll ask my mum.'

'Only... I've seen your photo albums,' said Jenny, 'and I don't remember any photos of a baby brother.'

Tim blushed.

'Terry doesn't exist, does he?' said Jenny.

Glossary

- **blushed:** turned pink with shame or embarrassment
- **his whereabouts:** where he is
- **muscular:** has a lot of muscles
- **skinny:** very thin
- **works out:** does exercise in the gym

CONFESSIONS

12 'So, really you are covering up• for William,' said Jenny.

'William broke the arch, not you. What about the twins?' said Jenny. 'Who gave you that idea?'

'Uncle Frank,' said Tim. 'I was in a panic so I invented Terry.'

'I feel I know Terry now as well as I know you,' said Jenny. 'I'd like to have him as a friend. What a pity he's so naughty!'

Jenny and Tim looked at each other and then they both started laughing.

'How did you know that Terry was an invention•?' said Tim.

'I know you too well,' said Jenny. 'You can't keep secrets from me, and... you can't keep secrets from your mum. Sooner or later she'll find out.'

'But what about Auntie Ruby... and Uncle Frank? She'll be so mad with them.'

'Take my advice and tell her,' said Jenny. 'She'll understand.'

Advice

What advice does Jenny give to Tim?
Do you think it is good advice?

With a partner think of advice for the following situations.

- ☐ One friend has no money.
- ☐ Another friend is always late for school.
- ☐ Another friend is getting very fat.

- **an invention:** not real
- **covering up:** keeping a secret (so William doesn't get into trouble)

THE HANDBAG INCIDENT

14 Tim walked towards the park. He was on his way to find Mr Thomas the gardener and apologise• to him. He wanted everything to be the way it was before.

He could hear a dog growling and barking in the distance. When he looked up, he saw Mrs Green and Bluebell on the path in front of him. Bluebell was attacking a tall thin man with dark hair. It took Tim a few moments to recognise him. It was the same man who crashed into him outside the gym. Bluebell was attacking the man because the man was trying to run away with Mrs Green's handbag.

Glossary

- **apologise:** say he is sorry

CONFESSIONS

12 'So, really you are covering up• for William,' said Jenny.

'William broke the arch, not you. What about the twins?' said Jenny. 'Who gave you that idea?'

'Uncle Frank,' said Tim. 'I was in a panic so I invented Terry.'

'I feel I know Terry now as well as I know you,' said Jenny. 'I'd like to have him as a friend. What a pity he's so naughty!'

Jenny and Tim looked at each other and then they both started laughing.

'How did you know that Terry was an invention•?' said Tim.

'I know you too well,' said Jenny. 'You can't keep secrets from me, and... you can't keep secrets from your mum. Sooner or later she'll find out.'

'But what about Auntie Ruby... and Uncle Frank? She'll be so mad with them.'

'Take my advice and tell her,' said Jenny. 'She'll understand.'

Advice

What advice does Jenny give to Tim?
Do you think it is good advice?

With a partner think of advice for the following situations.

- ☐ One friend has no money.
- ☐ Another friend is always late for school.
- ☐ Another friend is getting very fat.

- **an invention:** not real
- **covering up:** keeping a secret (so William doesn't get into trouble)

A SPECIAL SON

13 'Who's Terry?' said Mum as she unpacked her shopping.

'Terry? I don't know,' said Tim. He had made a large jam sandwich and was just about to bite into it.

'Maybe he goes to another school, not Arkwright,' said Mum. 'I heard some mothers talking about him in the supermarket today. He sounds awful. He's damaged property and he's stolen things. They think he's the mugger on all those posters.'

Tim didn't want to eat his jam sandwich any more.

'What else did they say?' said Tim.

'They blamed it on his parents,' she said. 'They must be doing something wrong. I agree with them.' She glanced• at Tim. 'Are you all right, darling? You look a bit pale.'

'I'm OK,' he said.

'You're working too hard on your project,' said Mum. She closed the fridge door. 'Come here and give me a hug,' she said. She put her arms around Tim and squeezed• him tightly.

'You are such a good boy,' she said. 'I know it wasn't easy for you after Dad and I divorced, but you're the best. You really are. You look after me. You look after Auntie Ruby, and you look after your uncle Frank. I'm so lucky to have a son like you. Poor Terry. His parents are probably very disappointed in him.'

Glossary

- **glanced:** looked quickly
- **squeezed:** held close

By the time Tim reached his room, he had tears in his eyes. He sat on the edge of his bed. He couldn't tell his mum. He just couldn't. He was so afraid of disappointing her.

'Hello Tim,' said a voice. 'Or should I say "Terry"?' It was Auntie Ruby. 'Guess what?' she said. 'Your uncle Frank says he wants a dog for company. What do you think? Is that a good idea?'

Tim didn't speak.

'Tim?' said Auntie Ruby. 'You're crying.'

'No, I've got something in my eye,' said Tim.

Auntie Ruby sat down next to him. She put her arm around his shoulder. 'What's the matter? You can tell me.'

Tim wiped his face with the back of his hand. 'Everybody is talking about Terry. They're saying what a bad person he is... and he's me.'

'Tim, I love both of you,' said Auntie Ruby, 'but stop feeling sorry for yourself and stop telling lies. You can't go on being two people. Just be yourself.'

Problems

How many people know Tim's secret? Who are they?
If you have a problem, who do you go to first for help?

- ☐ Your best friend?
- ☐ Your parents?
- ☐ Your brother or sister?
- ☐ Your teacher?

THE HANDBAG INCIDENT

14 Tim walked towards the park. He was on his way to find Mr Thomas the gardener and apologise• to him. He wanted everything to be the way it was before.

He could hear a dog growling and barking in the distance. When he looked up, he saw Mrs Green and Bluebell on the path in front of him. Bluebell was attacking a tall thin man with dark hair. It took Tim a few moments to recognise him. It was the same man who crashed into him outside the gym. Bluebell was attacking the man because the man was trying to run away with Mrs Green's handbag.

Glossary

- **apologise:** say he is sorry

'Hey, you!' shouted Tim.

Bluebell released the man's leg and barked at Tim. The man seized his chance and ran like the wind, with Mrs Green's handbag under his arm. Tim followed. He chased the man past some houses, then through a car park, then up a hill, then along the High Street, then through an open air café and past the library. Two girls stood outside the library with their mouths open.

'Did you see that? said Claire.

'It was Terry,' said Lynn.

'Or maybe it was Tim,' said Claire.

'No, it was Terry,' said Lynn. 'I'd know him anywhere.'

- **chased:** ran after; followed running
- **released:** let go of; freed
- **seized:** took; grabbed

THE MYSTERY HERO

15 Mrs Green had an important announcement to make. A group of newspaper reporters• waited outside her house. The door of the house opened and two policemen and a police inspector came out. Cameras flashed. A dog barked. The police inspector raised his hand for silence.

'We have caught a young man. He is helping us with our enquiries•. We believe he is the Wrightham mugger.'

The cameras flashed again.

'Who's the mystery hero?' shouted one of the reporters.

'What we know is this. A schoolboy chased after the suspect•. The suspect tripped• and dropped the stolen handbag. He also dropped his wallet•, and inside the wallet we found a gym membership card with the suspect's photograph and name on it. He made our job very easy.'

'Who's the schoolboy?' shouted a reporter. 'Is his name Terry?'

'We're not sure,' said the police inspector, 'but we want to give him a reward•.'

The crowd was quite large now and right in the middle were Tim, Jenny and William.

'Did you hear that, Tim?' said William. 'There's a reward. Tell them you chased the mugger. Tell them you're Terry.'

'I'm Tim,' said Tim. 'I'm not Terry.'

But William was already talking to one of the reporters.

Glossary

- **enquiries:** questions
- **reporters:** journalists
- **reward:** money; prize
- **suspect:** person police think was the mugger
- **tripped:** fell over
- **wallet:** small case for holding paper money

'Excuse me, excuse me,' he said. 'This is the boy. He helped Mrs Green.' Just then the front door of the house opened and Mrs Green stepped out. The reporters bombarded• her with questions.

'I just want to say one thing,' she said. 'A brave young man helped me. I am grateful• to him and if I find him, I'll give him a reward.'

Tim felt someone's hand on his shoulder. It was the reporter. He pushed Tim through the crowd until he stood in front of Mrs Green.

'Is this him? Is this the mystery hero?' said the reporter.

The people in the crowd looked and listened. Mrs Green adjusted• her glasses and looked at Tim very carefully. Bluebell sniffed• at his feet, then sat looking at Tim with her tail wagging•.

'My goodness,' said Mrs Green, 'you look just like him!'

A murmur• went through the crowd.

'But,' said Mrs Green, 'I think he was taller, his hair was darker, and he was more muscular.'

'It's not him?' said the reporter.

'No,' said Mrs Green, 'it's not.'

There was a disturbance in the crowd. A boy pushed his way to the front. It was William. 'I saved Mrs Green,' he said. 'It was me!'

Mrs Green leaned forward and looked closely at William. 'I am old,' she said, 'and my memory is poor, but I know you very well, William. And it was not you!'

- **adjusted:** moved (them) to see more clearly
- **bombarded:** asked one question after another
- **grateful:** happy and thankful
- **murmur:** low sound
- **sniffed:** smelled closely with his nose
- **wagging:** moving quickly up and down

SUMMER IN WRIGHTHAM

16 No one came forward to get the reward. And fewer and fewer people 'saw' Terry. Some children said Terry was in prison. Other children said he was in California. William said he was on an expedition climbing Mount Everest. Tim said he was overseas in a secret place with his dad.

In the local newspapers there were reports of the handbag incident, but Mum never read them. She didn't have time. She was very busy in the summer term. She taught her computing classes and she studied for her university exams. And Tim hid the newspapers.

Uncle Frank moved into his new house, worked on his garden, and joined the Wrightham Seniors' Social Club. He made lots of friends and told everyone stories of his identical twin. Sometimes his twin's name was Wilfred and sometimes it was Dennis. Uncle Frank's stories were not always accurate.

Auntie Ruby returned to her job in Scotland, but she visited her father every second weekend. Auntie Ruby and Tim did the shopping while Mum did her exam preparation. It worked out very well.

Tim kept Arkwright tidy through his KAT project. The rest of the time he planned his trip to Disneyland. Jenny decorated Arkwright's walls and open spaces with student art. Then she did the same in Wrightham General Hospital and organised painting lessons for the children in the hospital. William worked on his Citizens' Aid project. Because he was so lazy, he only aided one citizen – Mrs Green.

Everyone looked forward to Arkwright's Summer Open Day. That was the day when Mrs Barrow was going to announce the winner of the Arkwright School Student of the Year Award.

Write a quiz

Write five questions about summer in Wrightham. Ask your partner to answer the questions

AND THE WINNER IS...

17 'I've just met a charming• lady,' said Uncle Frank. 'Her name is Mrs Green. She has a dog called Bluebell.'

The children groaned•.

'What's Mrs Green doing here?' said William. 'She and her horrible dog should be at home. Doesn't she know this is a special day for us?'

The students were excited and a little bit nervous. Mrs Barrow was about to announce the winner of the Student of the Year Award. Tim's mum, his uncle Frank and his auntie Ruby were waiting with the other parents and relatives to hear the result.

Student of the Year

Who deserves• to win the Student of the Year Award?

Talk to your partner and choose the winner.
Tell the class who you chose and why.

'There are some great projects – like yours, Tim,' said Jenny. 'And there are some really bad projects. Did you hear about Claire and Lynn? Mrs Barrow eliminated• them.'

'Why?' said Tim. He looked around for Claire. She was sitting next to her mother. She looked very unhappy.

Glossary

- **charming:** kind; with good manners
- **deserves:** is the right person
- **eliminated:** removed them from the competition
- **groaned:** made a noise to say they were unhappy

'They did a reading project for kids from the local primary schools,' said Jenny.

'What's wrong with that?' said Tim.

'They read horror stories to the children and the parents complained,' said William.

'I hope you win, Tim,' said Jenny. 'You deserve a prize for hiding Terry from your mum.'

'Yes, how many newspapers did you hide?' said William.

'Welcome, everyone, to the Arkwright School Open Day,' said Mrs Barrow. She was at the microphone. 'Before I announce the winner of our Student of the Year Award, I would like to introduce to you – at last – our anonymous• benefactor•. It is Mrs Margaret Green.'

Mrs Green stood up, smiled and gave a little bow•.

'Oh, no!' said William and he held his head in his hands.

'Well, well, well!' said Uncle Frank looking very pleased with himself. 'I knew she was special when I saw she had a dog.'

Mrs Green addressed the audience. 'I'd like to thank all the students of Arkwright for their wonderful projects,' she said. 'You have worked very hard. You will all get certificates. William, will you please stand up. William, your Citizens' Aid project, helping old people in the community, is brilliant. You helped at least one old person. Me. Thank you very much. Now, with my help, you can develop• your project and help other senior citizens like me. I have a list of all the old people you can visit. You can start tomorrow.'

William sat down, stunned•.

Glossary

- **anonymous:** without a name; hiding their identity
- **benefactor:** person who does good things or gives something
- **bow:** bent the top of her body
- **develop:** extend; expand
- **stunned:** shocked

'Tim,' said Mrs Green. 'Will you please stand up?'

Tim stood up. His heart beat very fast.

'I cannot praise you enough, Tim,' said Mrs Green. 'Arkwright School is clean and organised thanks to you.'

Tim waited. Nothing happened.

'But now for the winner,' said Mrs Green. 'The award goes to Jenny Slater for her wonderful Arkwright Art project. Congratulations, Jenny!'

Jenny turned to look at Tim. 'Tim...' she began.

Tim interrupted her. 'Jenny,' he said, 'I'm sad I lost, but I'm glad you won.'

Tim was pleased for Jenny, but he was also very disappointed.

Losing

Why is Tim disappointed about not winning the Award?

What does it feel like when you don't win?

Think of a time when you were disappointed.

What happened? How did you react?

Tell a partner.

'You can try again next year,' said Mum.

'You don't understand,' said Tim. 'You won't get your holiday.'

'Don't worry about me,' said Mum. 'Every day's a holiday with you.'

'But,' said Tim, and he went white.

'What's the matter, Tim?' said Mum.

Mrs Barrow was walking towards them through the crowd of students and parents.

'It's time to go home now, Mum,' said Tim.

Mrs Barrow walked up to Auntie Ruby and took her hand.

'Mrs Norris,' she said. 'It's so nice to see you again.'

Auntie Ruby turned pale. Mum looked at Auntie Ruby and then at Tim. Tim bit his lip and looked at the ground.

'And how is Tim's twin, Terry?' said Mrs Barrow. 'No one has seen him. There's a reward waiting for him.'

'He's gone away,' said Auntie Ruby.

'Ah, that explains it,' said Mrs Barrow.

'Yes, he and his father are living in New York,' said Auntie Ruby. 'His father got a job there.'

'Oh, very good,' said Mrs Barrow. 'Is he working as an airline pilot or as a travel writer?'

'A travel writer,' said Tim.

'An airline pilot,' said Auntie Ruby.

Auntie Ruby glared at Tim, and Tim glared at Auntie Ruby.

'So,' said Mum, when Mrs Barrow left to join the other parents. 'Now you can both tell me all about Terry.'

MUM'S SECRET

18 Tim and his mum walked side by side in the park. It was the first week of the summer holidays.

'I have a confession• to make,' said Mum. 'I've kept a secret from you.'

'Mum?' said Tim.

'Auntie Ruby and I are going on holiday.'

'But I thought we didn't have any money,' said Tim. 'How can we afford• a holiday?'

'Tim, look around you,' said Mum. 'I've got a job. Auntie Ruby has a great job in Scotland. Uncle Frank has a beautiful house here in Wrightham, and your dad sends us a cheque• every month. I think we can afford a holiday.'

They sat down on a bench opposite the rose garden.

'What a beautiful arch,' said Mum. 'I've never noticed it before.'

'Yes, it's new,' said Tim.

'You know,' said Mum. 'I'm proud of you for trying to win us a holiday, but we can pay for our own holiday. Auntie Ruby and I are going to Paris to visit the art galleries and the museums and eat good food, but – best of all – we're going shopping.'

'So, do you want me to look after Uncle Frank?' said Tim.

'Yes, I do. I want you to look after him and I want you to take him to Disneyland,' said Mum. 'Do you think you can do that? Jenny can help you. She'll be there with her family at the same time and I won't be far away. Disneyland is just twenty miles from the centre of Paris'

Tim blinked•. 'Are you serious?' he said.

Glossary

- **afford:** have enough money for
- **blinked:** closed and opened his eyes (here, because he is surprised)
- **cheque:** like money
- **confession:** when you tell the truth

'I'm serious,' said Mum. 'There's just one condition.' She looked very serious.

'What do you mean, Mum?' said Tim.

'You must promise me something,' said Mum. 'This bad twin Terry... your brother, my naughty son... and Uncle Frank's twin Wilfred or Dennis, or whatever he is called... you must leave them both behind. I refuse to pay for their holiday and I'm not going to buy two sets of clothes ever again.'

'Don't worry, Mum. I promise. We'll leave them both behind forever.'

After Reading

Personal Response

1 Answer these questions with a partner.

a) Did you like the story? Why? Why not?

b) Did you learn any new words? Tell your partner at least five new words that you learned. Who learned the most words?

c) Was there any part of the story that you didn't understand? Ask your partner about it.

d) What did you think of Tim? Did you like him best or did you like another character better? Tell your partner.

e) What do you think about Tim's friends? Would you like to make friends with any of them? Who?

f) Would you like to be a character from the story? Which character would you like to be?

g) Did you guess the ending of the story? Was the ending a surprise or not? Together think of a different ending.

h) Do you think *Twins* was a good title for the story? Can you think of a better title?

After Reading

Comprehension

1 Are the following sentences true (T) or false (F)? Tick (✔).

	T	F
a) The winner of the Student of the Year Award will get a family ticket for Disneyland Paris.	☐	☐
b) Tim's mum teaches science at the local college.	☐	☐
c) Uncle Frank is moving to a new house in Scotland.	☐	☐
d) Ruby is Uncle Frank's daughter.	☐	☐
e) Uncle Frank didn't have an identical twin.	☐	☐
f) Someone took the pencil case that contained Tim's money and his favourite pen.	☐	☐
g) William carried Mrs Green's shopping basket for her in the supermarket.	☐	☐
h) Tim broke the arch at the entrance to the rose garden.	☐	☐
i) Mr Thomas is a gardener.	☐	☐
j) Tim has an identical twin brother who is called Terry.	☐	☐
k) Mrs Barrow wanted to speak to Tim's twin brother.	☐	☐
l) Auntie Ruby pretends to be Tim's mother.	☐	☐
m) Tim's mum paid for the broken arch.	☐	☐
n) Jenny's project is called 'Reading for Kids'.	☐	☐
o) Mrs Barrow finds out that Auntie Ruby is not Tim's mother.	☐	☐
p) Tim and Uncle Frank will take their twins with them to Disneyland, Paris.	☐	☐

2 Match the two halves of the sentences about the story.

a) ☐ Tim is a teenager
b) ☐ William breaks the arch in the park
c) ☐ Tim tells a lie to the Head Teacher
d) ☐ Terry is the identical twin brother
e) ☐ Tim does not claim the reward for helping Mrs Green

1 because he wants to be Student of the Year.
2 that Tim invents to get himself out of trouble.
3 because he wants to be himself, not Terry.
4 who wants to win an award and take his mother on a special holiday.
5 but Tim gets the blame.

3 When does Tim say the following? Match his words with the situations below.

a) ☐ 'I've got something in my eye.'
b) ☐ 'So, do you want me to look after Uncle Frank?'
c) ☐ 'I was in a panic so I invented Terry.'
d) ☐ 'I'm sad I lost, but I'm glad you won.'
e) ☐ 'It's time to go home now, Mum.'
f) ☐ 'I'm Tim. I'm not Terry.'

1 When he doesn't want Mum to meet Mrs Barrow.
2 When Mrs Green offers a reward to the boy who helped her.
3 After Mum says she is going on a holiday with Auntie Ruby.
4 After Jenny wins the Student of the Year Award.
5 When Auntie Ruby finds him crying.
6 When he tells Jenny about his meeting with Mrs Barrow and Mr Thomas.

After Reading

Characters

1 **How do the characters from *Twins* feel in the following situations? Choose words from the box.**

suspicious	stressed	stunned	embarrassed	confused	angry

a) When Mr Thomas saw a boy running across his grass, he was ....

b) When Mrs Barrow hears for the first time about Tim's twin brother, she is ....

c) William is .... when Mrs Green asks him to help other senior citizens.

d) When Mrs Green finds cat food in her shopping trolley, she is ....

e) Auntie Ruby is .... when Mrs Barrow questions her about Terry.

f) Tim is .... when Jenny finds out he is lying about his twin brother.

2 **Who says this? What do we learn about their character from what they say? Is there anything we can learn about life in general from what they say?**

a) 'You know, I'd like to be Student of the Year myself, but I'm far too old for that now.'

b) 'I'm impressed with Tim's project. I don't think mine is as good as that.'

c) 'We feel a bit sorry for you because your ideas are so pathetic.'

d) 'I don't need to go to Disneyland to have fun. I can have lots of fun here at home.'

e) 'You're working too hard on your project. Come here and give me a hug.'

3 Write the names of the characters beside the sentences.

a) She's good at ice skating. She starts an art club at school. ....

b) She lives in Wrightham, but her cousin lives in Scotland. ....

c) She has a powerful voice. She has a new job in Wrightham. ....

d) He was a troublemaker when he was young. His daughter has a great job. ....

e) He's good at running. He rides a bicycle. His parents are divorced and he lives with his mother. ....

4 Write some facts about three of the characters from Twins. Ask a partner to read your sentences and guess the character.

5 Work in groups of four. Imagine that you are helping Mrs Barrow and Mr Thomas to find out more about Terry and the incident in the park.

a) Write down questions you want to ask William, Jenny and Tim.

b) Find three students to be William, Jenny and Tim. Ask them to leave the room.

c) Write down what you think their answers will be to the questions.

d) Call William, Jenny and Tim back into the room. Ask them your questions.

e) Did they give the answers you wrote down?

After Reading

Plot and Theme

1 Which of these themes can you find in *Twins*? Tick (✔).

- ☐ The importance of caring for others
- ☐ The beauty of nature
- ☐ Honesty and dishonesty
- ☐ Memory
- ☐ Friendship
- ☐ Loneliness
- ☐ Loyalty

2 There are many stories or sub-plots in *Twins*. Find two sentences below that describe the stories of Jenny, Auntie Ruby and William.

a) She starts up an art project at her school, then wins the Student of the Year Award.

b) He breaks the arch in the rose garden but lets Tim take the blame.

c) She is helping her father move into a new house. Tim makes her pretend to be his mother.

d) Mrs Green praises him for his Citizens' Aid project then gives him a list of old people to visit.

e) She and Tim's mother book a holiday in Paris for themselves, and one for Tim and Uncle Frank.

f) She goes with her family to Disneyland Paris and meets up with Tim and his family.

3 Work with a partner. Choose a character or characters from the list below and summarise their story in a just a few sentences.

a) Mrs Green b) Claire and Lynn c) The Wrightham Mugger

4 Work with a partner. Do you agree with any of these statements? If possible, find examples in the story to support your answers.

a) One lie always leads to another lie.

b) Your mother always finds out if you have done something wrong.

c) There is good and bad in everyone.

d) You should help your friends by covering up their mistakes.

e) There is no need to tell your secrets to your best friend.

5 Here are twelve things that happen in the story. Put them in the order that they happen.

1	2	3	4	5	6	7	8	9	10	11	12
a											l

a) Mrs Barrow announces the Arkwright School Student of the Year Award.

b) Jenny guesses that Tim does not have a twin brother.

c) Mr Thomas accuses Tim of breaking the arch.

d) Jenny wins the Student of the Year Award.

e) Mrs Green promises to reward the boy who helped her.

f) Auntie Ruby pretends to be Tim's mother.

g) Tim's mother finds out about Terry.

h) Tim tells Mrs Barrow he has a twin brother.

i) A mugger steals Tim's money.

j) Mrs Green is attacked by the Wrightham Mugger.

k) William breaks the arch in the rose garden.

l) Tim's mother and Auntie Ruby organise a family holiday in Paris.

After Reading

Language

1 **Read Tim's diary and answer the questions. Try to write complete sentences.**

SUNDAY 6	7 am	go for a run
	11:30 am	swimming with William
MONDAY 7	4 pm	meet Mum – Parkside Fitness Centre
TUESDAY 8		Work on KAT project
		Study for Maths test
WEDNESDAY 9	10 am	Maths test
		write KAT proposal
THURSDAY 10	4 pm	watch football
FRIDAY 11	5 pm	help Mum with shopping
	6 pm	watch DVD at William's house
SATURDAY 12	11 am	unpack Uncle Frank's boxes
	1 pm	lunch with Auntie Ruby and Uncle Frank
	3 pm	meet William and Jenny at ice rink

a) Why is Tim going to William's house on Friday?
He's watching a DVD there.

b) Why is he not going straight home after school on Thursday?

c) What is he doing on Sunday morning?

d) When are William and Jenny meeting at the ice rink?

e) What is Tim doing before lunch on Saturday?

f) When are Tim and Mum going shopping?

g) Why can't Tim go to William's house after school on Monday?

h) How many evenings during the week is Tim working on his KAT project?

2 **Work with a partner. Write a page from the diary of one of the characters from *Twins*. Write five questions about the diary and give the diary and the questions to another pair of students to answer.**

3 Jenny has made a list of all the things she has to do this weekend. Write sentences about what she *has* or *hasn't done*.

She hasn't tidied her bedroom yet.
She has already prepared for the Physics test.

- tidy bedroom ✗
- prepare for the Physics test ✓
- design an Arkwright Art publicity poster ✓
- do the shopping for Mum ✗
- make an appointment at the hairdresser ✓
- buy new sports bag ✗
- download music onto MP3 player ✗
- tidy History notes ✓
- finish the book report for English homework ✗

4 What have you done this week? Write as many things as you can think of in five minutes.

5 Complete these sentences. Choose the correct verb form.

a) William .... his project proposal yet. (didn't write/hasn't written)
b) Uncle Frank .... an action movie on TV last night. (watched/has watched)
c) William .... the arch in the rose garden last week. (broke/has broken)
d) Tim .... cornflakes for breakfast this morning. (had/has had)
e) Tim's father .... to New York about eight years ago. (moved/has moved)
f) Jenny .... four paintings already for her Arkwright Art project. (collected/has collected)

After Reading

Exit Test

1 Listen and choose (✔) the correct picture.

a) What does Tim give Uncle Frank?

☐ 1 ☐ 2 ☐ 3

b) Which sport seems dangerous to Tim?

☐ 1 ☐ 2 ☐ 3

c) What did the mugger steal from Tim?

☐ 1 ☐ 2 ☐ 3

d) What does Jenny ask Tim about?

☐ 1 ☐ 2 ☐ 3

K 2 Read the sentences about the story and choose the best word (1, 2, or 3) for each space.

a) Tim chased after a ....
1 dog 2 mugger 3 football

b) Tim ran across the damp grass and trampled Mr Thomas's ....
1 flowers 2 arch 3 sandwich

c) Tim says his father is ....
1 a teacher 2 a gardener 3 an airline pilot

d) Tim says his mother buys .... of everything.
1 one 2 two 3 three

e) The accusations against Terry .... Tim.
1 pleased 2 annoyed 3 upset

f) Tim was afraid of .... his mother so he didn't tell her about his lies.
1 surprising 2 stressing 3 disappointing

g) Tim didn't want to claim the ....
1 reward 2 award 3 gym membership card

K 3 Look at the picture on page 56 with a partner. Ask and answer questions about it.

How many people are there?

I think there are...

After Reading

Projects

1 **Complete this proposal sheet for Tim's Keep Arkwright Tidy project.**

Project Title

KAT (Keep Arkwright Tidy)

Aim of the Project

Who will benefit from your project? ....

How will they benefit? ....

The Project Team

Who will work with you on your project? ....

What jobs will they do? ....

Project Duration

How long will your project take to complete? ....

How many hours will you work on it each week? ....

Project Plan

What is your plan of action? ....

What will you do first, second, and third to achieve your aim? ....

Publicity

How will you advertise your project? ....

2 **Now work in a small group. Think of a project that will benefit your school or the local community. Write a proposal for your project.**